AND I
MEAN IT,
STANLEY

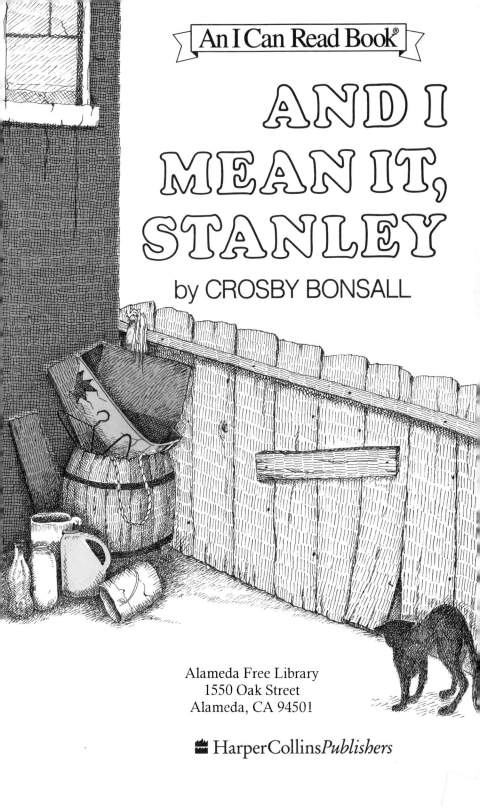

AND I MEAN IT, STANLEY

by CROSBY BONSALL

HarperCollins*Publishers*

And I Mean It, Stanley
Copyright © 1974 by Crosby Bonsall
All rights reserved. Printed in the United States of America.

Library of Congress Catalog Card Number: 73-14324
ISBN 0-06-020567-9
ISBN 0-06-020568-7 (lib. bdg.)
ISBN 0-06-444046-X (pbk.)

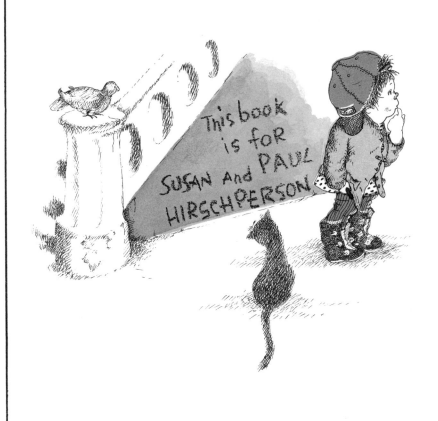

This book
is for
SUSAN and PAUL
HIRSCHPERSON

Listen, Stanley.

I know you are there.

I know you are

in back of the fence.

But I don't care, Stanley.

I don't want to play with you.

I don't want to talk to you.

You stay there, Stanley.

Stay in back of the fence.

I don't care.

I can play by myself, Stanley.

I don't need you, Stanley.

And I mean it, Stanley.

I am having a lot of fun.

A lot of fun!

I am making a great thing, Stanley.

A really, truly great thing.

And when it is done,

you will want to see it, Stanley.

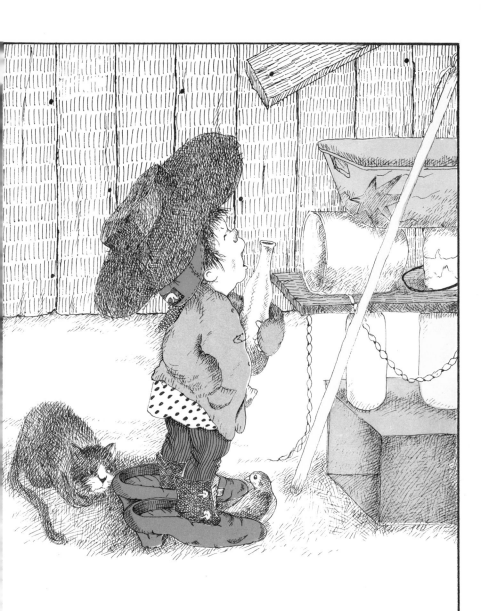

Well, you can't.

I don't want you to.

And I mean it, Stanley.

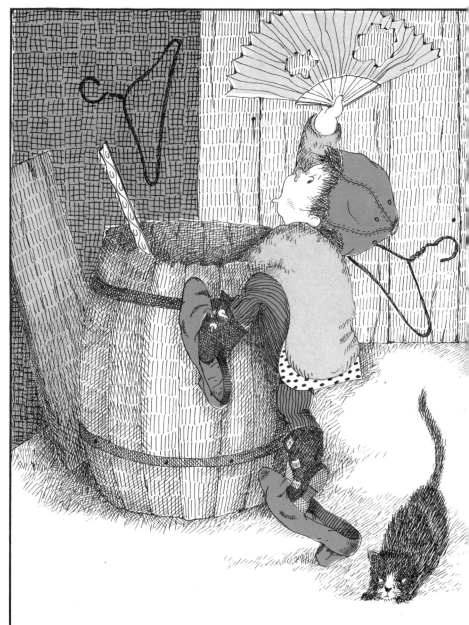

I don't want you to see

what I am making.

You stay there, Stanley.

Don't you look.

Don't you look.

Don't even peek.

You hear me, Stanley?

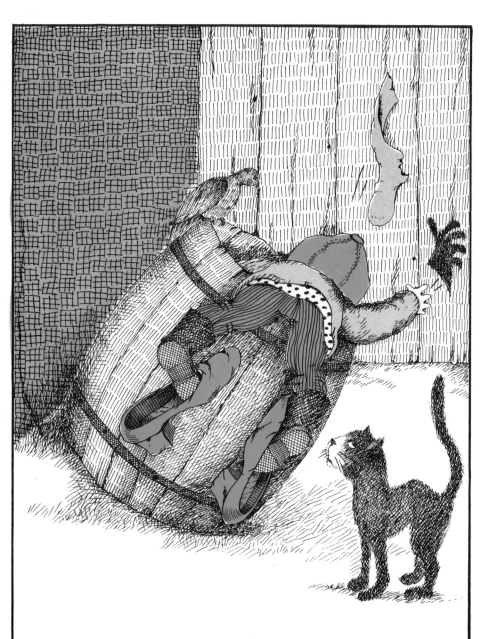

This thing I am making

is really neat.

It is really neat, Stanley.

And it is all made now.

The very best thing I ever made.

But don't you look, Stanley.

I don't want you to see it.

And I mean it...

STANLEY!

Aw, Stanley.